Simon and the Better Bone

by Corey R. Tabor

Balzer + Bray
An Imprint of HarperCollins Publishers

For Fido, Fluffy, and Spot

Balzer + Bray is an imprint of HarperCollins Publishers.

Simon and the Better Bone
Copyright © 2023 by Corey R. Tabor
All rights reserved. Manufactured in Italy.
No part of this book may be used or reproduced in any manner whatsoever without
written permission except in the case of brief quotations embodied in critical articles
and reviews. For information address HarperCollins Children's Books, a division of
HarperCollins Publishers, 195 Broadway, New York, NY 10007.
www.harpercollinschildrens.com

Library of Congress Control Number: 2022941732
ISBN 978-0-06-327555-3

The artist used pencil, colored pencil, and acrylic paint, assembled digitally,
to create the illustrations for this book.
Typography by Dana Fritts

RILO   10 9 8 7 6 5 4 3 2 1

Author's Note

Simon and the Better Bone is based on
Aesop's "The Dog and His Reflection."
But Simon gets a happier ending (he is
a good boy, after all).

Simon was out playing by the pond when he found a bone. If there was a better bone in all the world, Simon hadn't seen it.

But then he spotted
something in the pond.

It was another bone.
A *better* bone.

There was a dog holding the bone. But it was a scrawny little dog. Certainly no match for Simon.

But Simon was a good boy.

"Hello!" he said to the other dog.

"Would you like to trade bones?"

The other dog didn't reply.

How rude! Clearly this was one of those *bad dogs* you hear about.

"I challenge you to a staring contest!"
said Simon. "Winner gets the better bone!"

Simon wiggled his nose.
He opened his eyes really big.
He crossed them.

But the other dog
knew the same tricks.

Simon tried his other tricks. He chased his tail. He played dead. He recited his favorite poem. He chased his tail while playing dead while reciting his favorite poem.

But the other dog knew those tricks too.

Simon issued
a polite warning.

grrrrr

Then he pounced.

ARF!
ARF!
ARF!
ARF!
ARF!

The better bone will be MINE!

thought Simon.

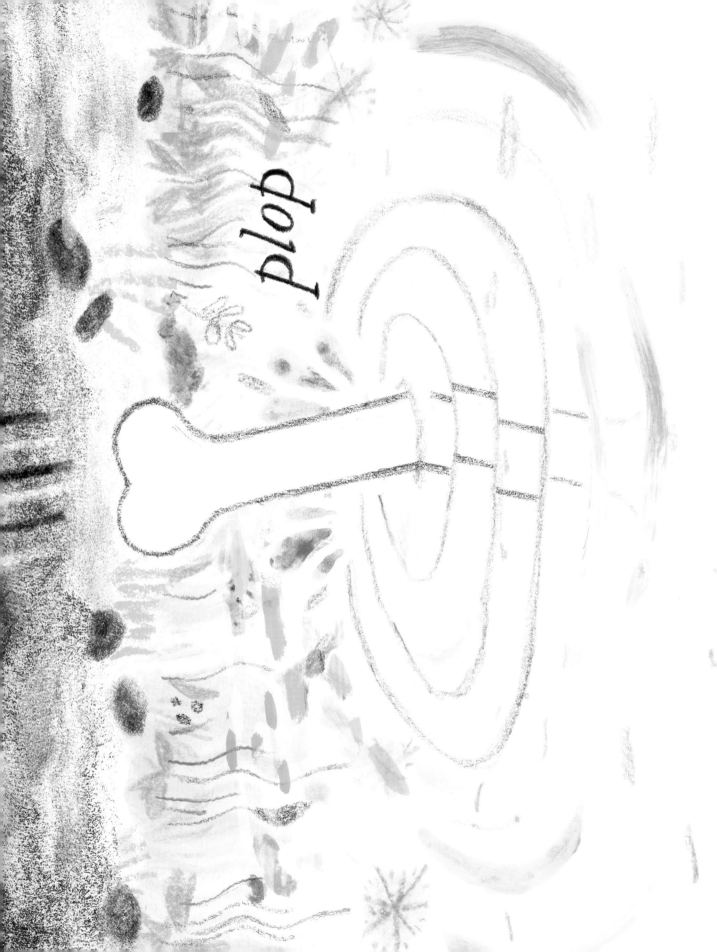

plop

"I see that you've lost your bone too," said Simon.

Simon thought about saying sorry. But then he spotted something over in the dirt.

It was a bone.
A *better* better bone.

There was only
one thing to do.

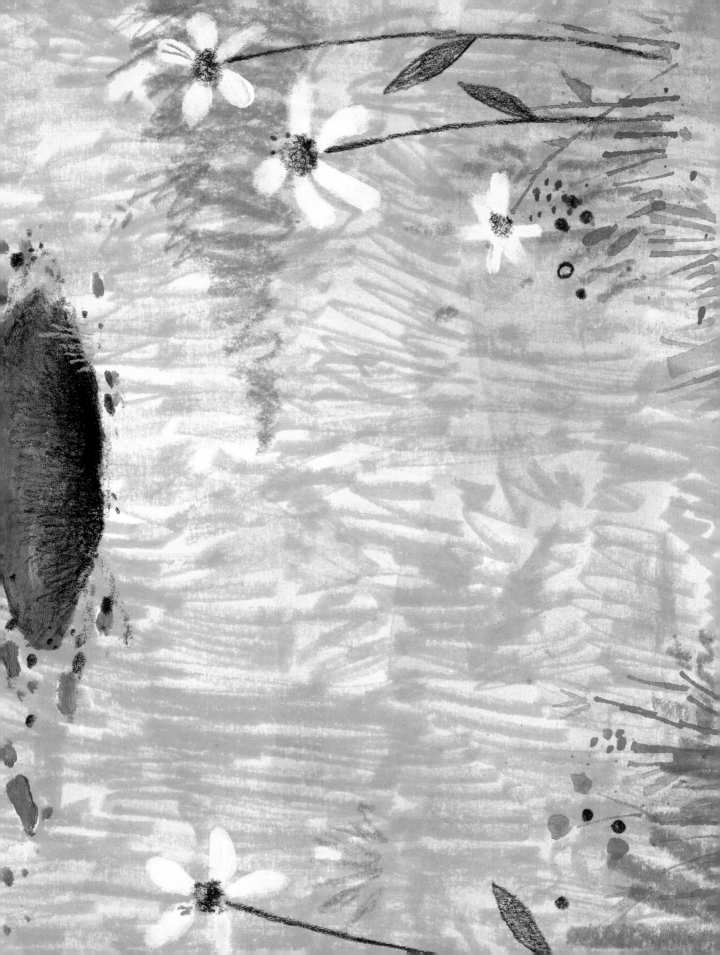

"Here!" said Simon.

"This is for you!"

The other dog wagged his tail and disappeared with the bone.

Simon smiled. He'd lost a bone,
but he'd found a friend.

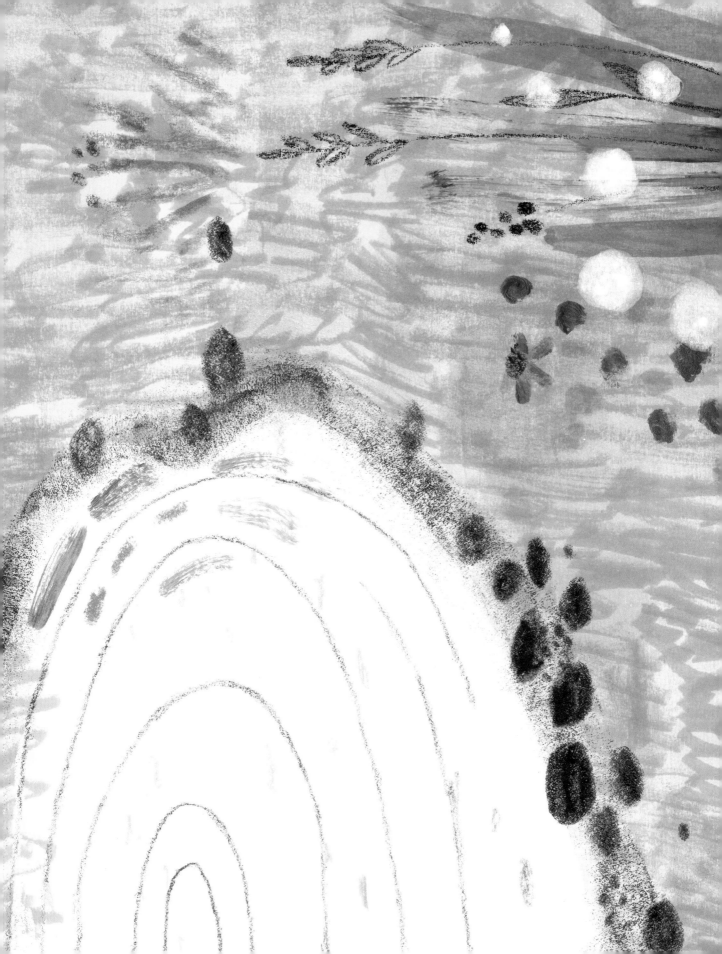

I hope I see him again soon, thought Simon.